**RELAXING COLORS**
PRESS

Copyright © 2022

Publication by Relaxing Colors Press

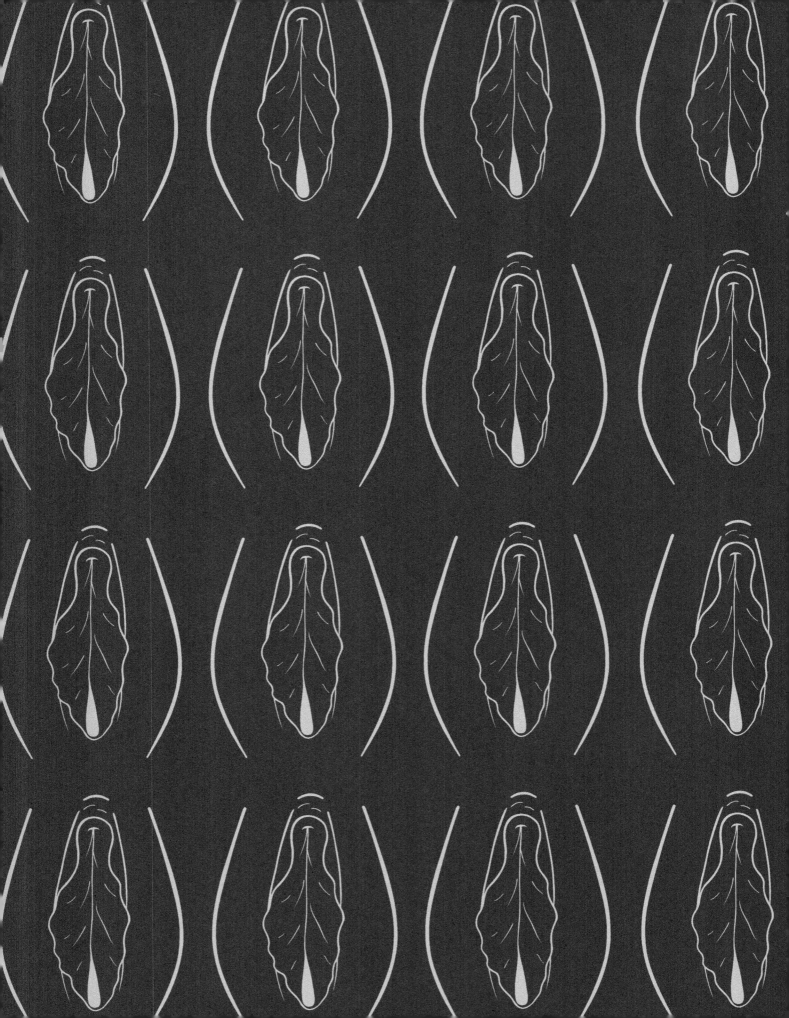

# This Vagina Book Belongs to:

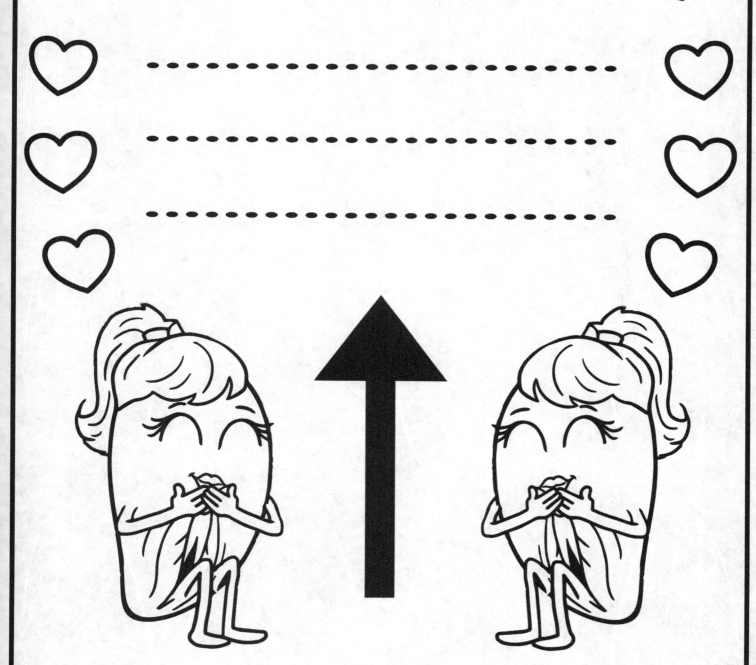

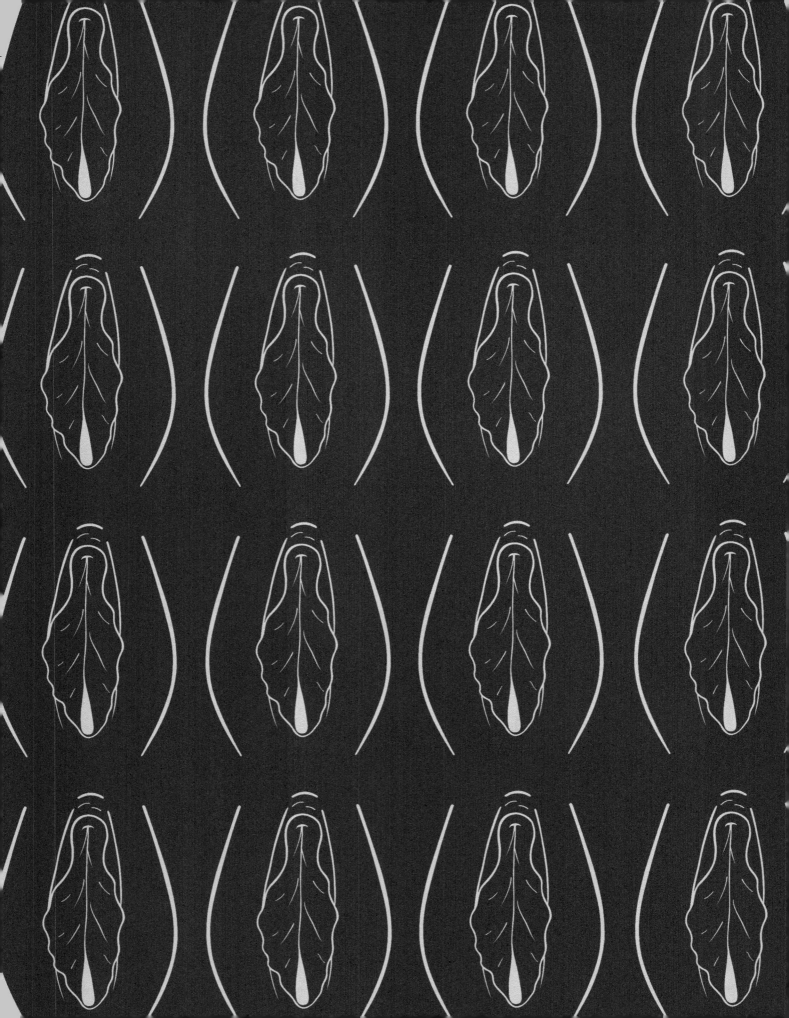

# THANK YOU FOR YOUR SUPPORT!

This fun coloring book, designed specifically for adults with a sense of humor, is an excellent way to relax and spend quality time without technology like tv, phones, etc.

Coloring is a great way to escape any problems and enter the world of colors, so I hope you will enjoy the designs and they will make you smile.

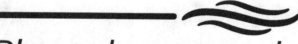

## Please leave your honest review.

*It helps me to improve myself and create better coloring books.*

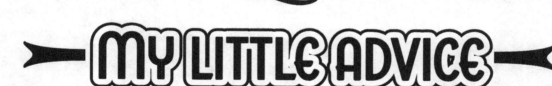

# MY LITTLE ADVICE

Each image is placed on a separate page to reduce the problem of color bleeding.

But you can always put an extra piece of paper under each page you color to ensure everything goes your way.

Thank you.

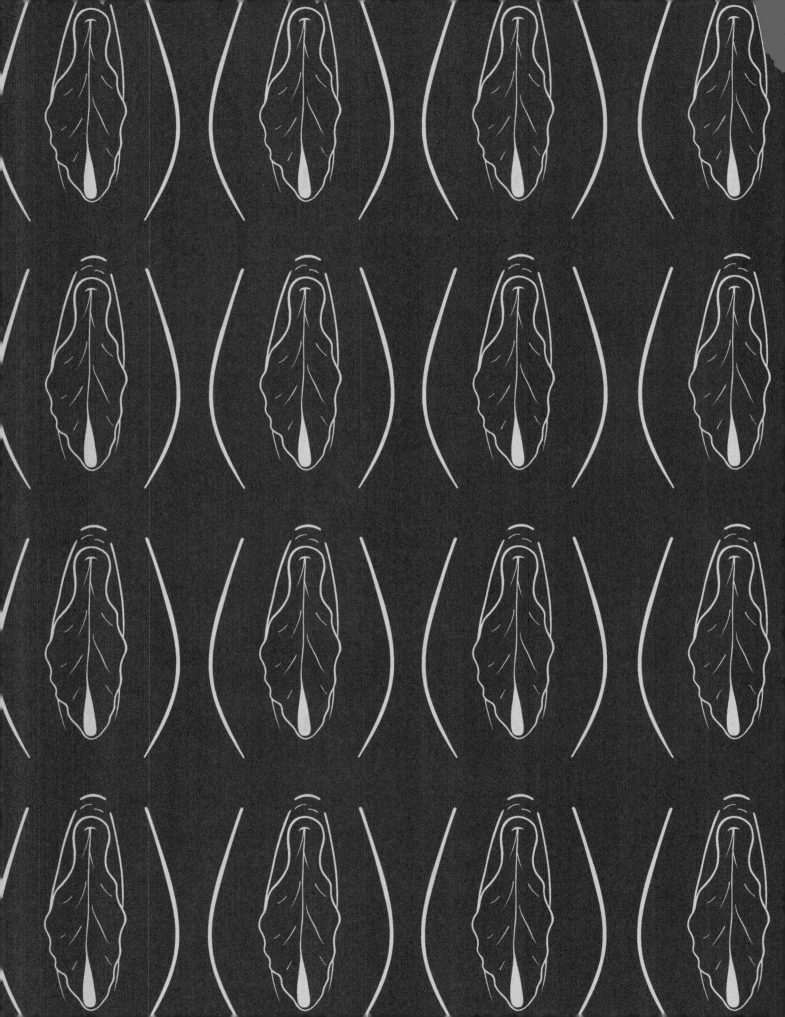

# TESTING PAGE

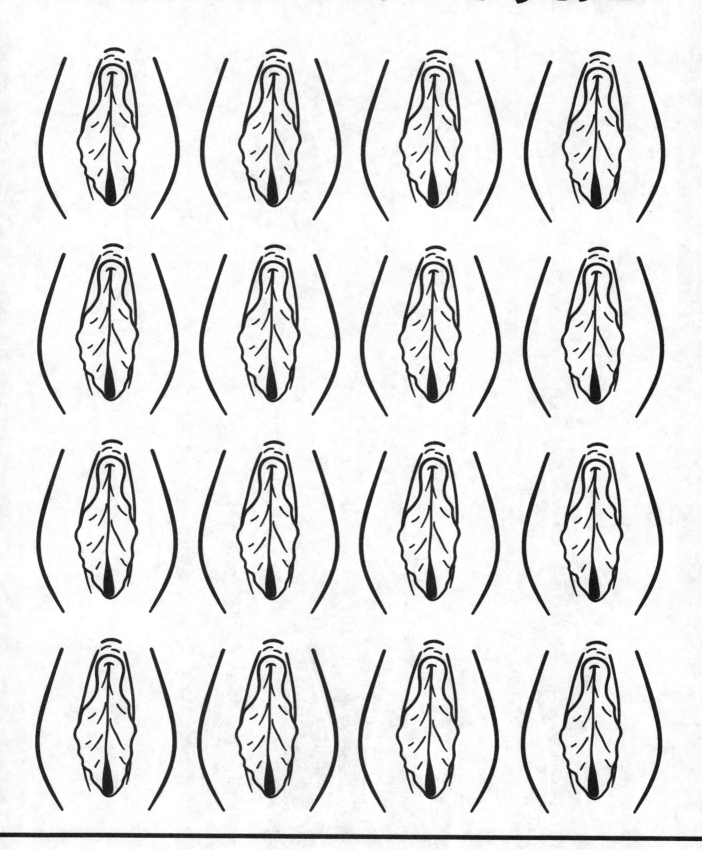

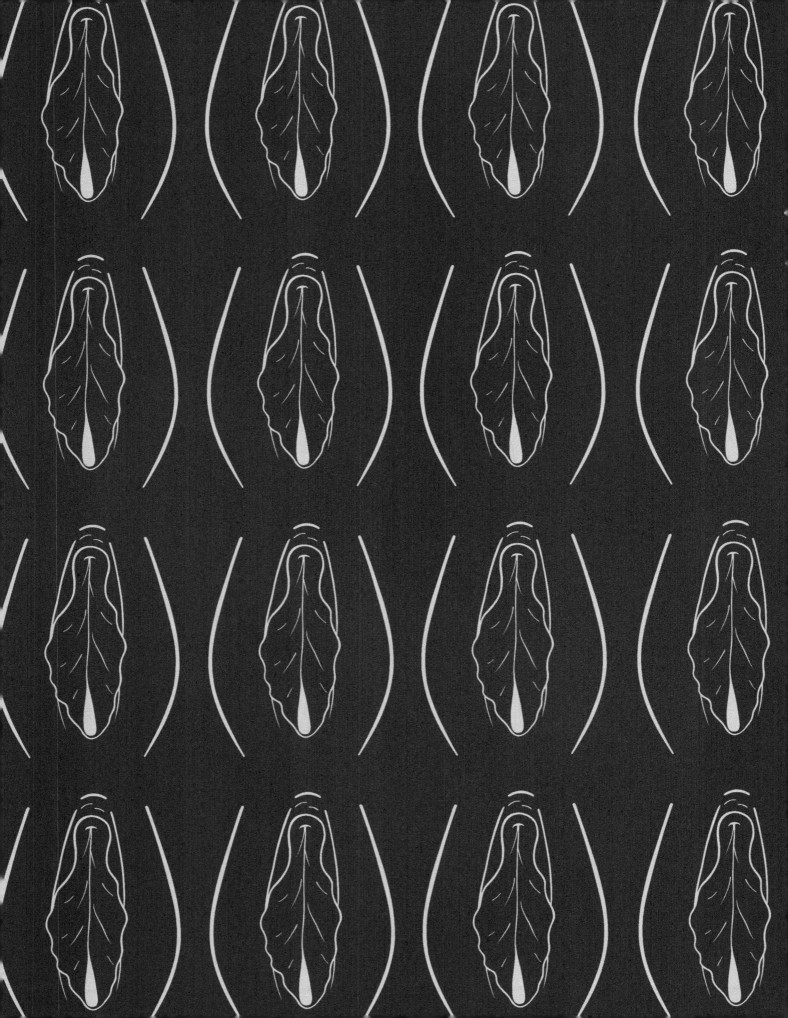

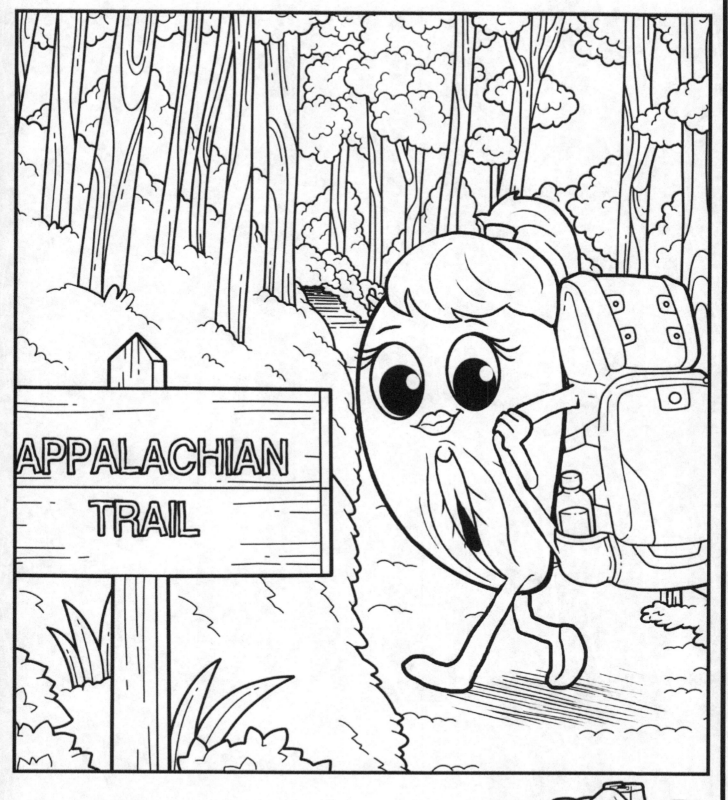

# HIKING THE APPALACHIAN TRAIL

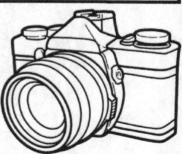

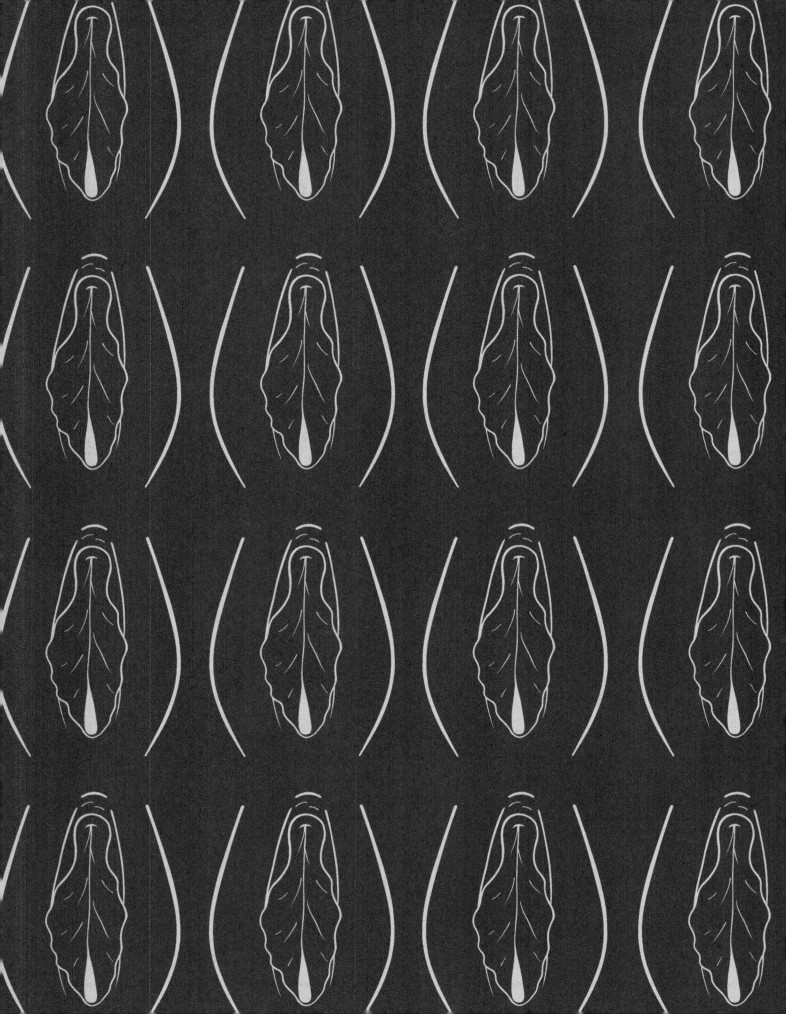

# SKYDIVING

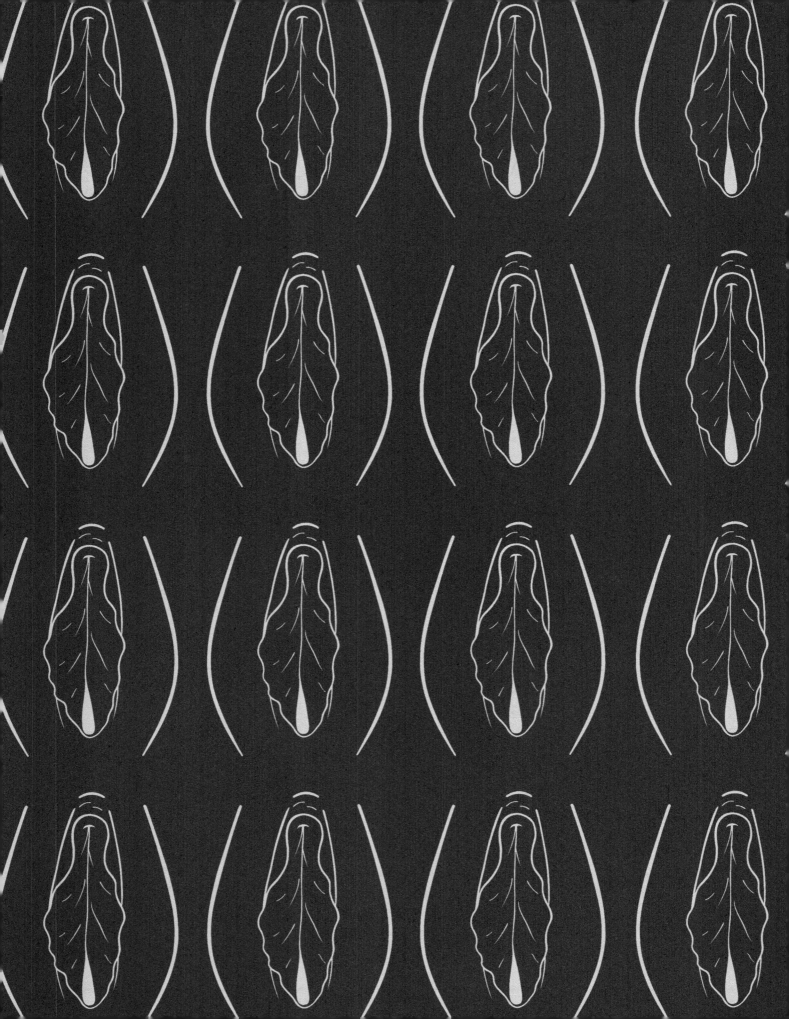

# RACING CARS

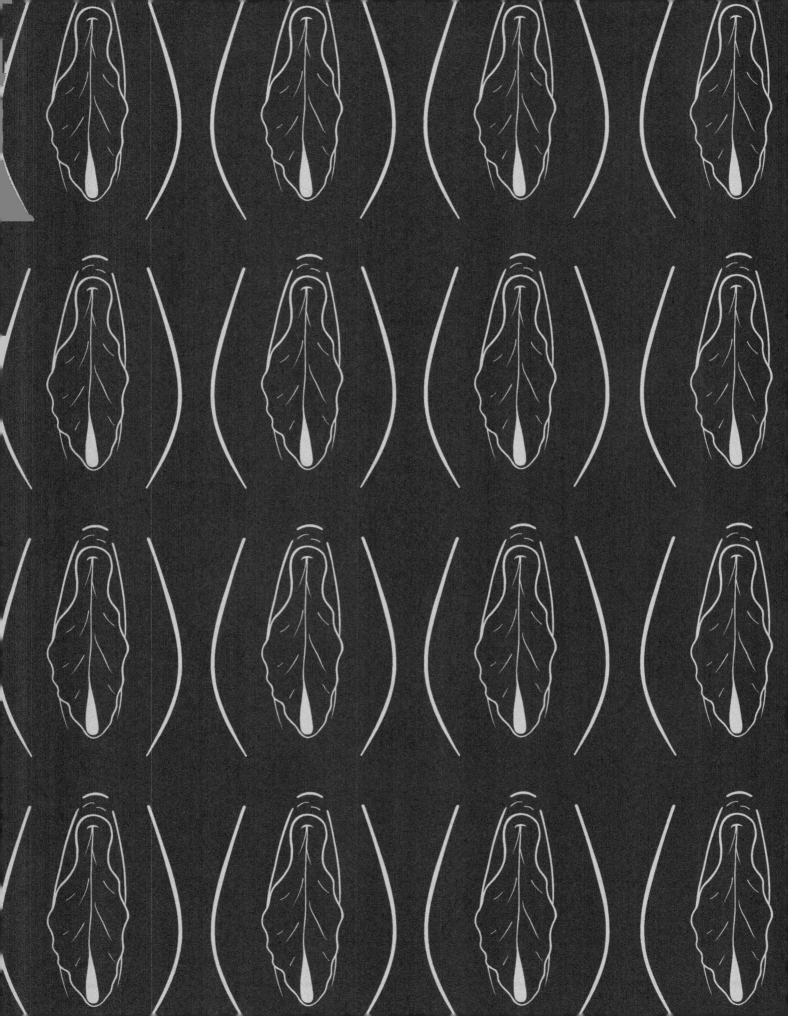

# DOUBLE DUTCH JUMP ROPE

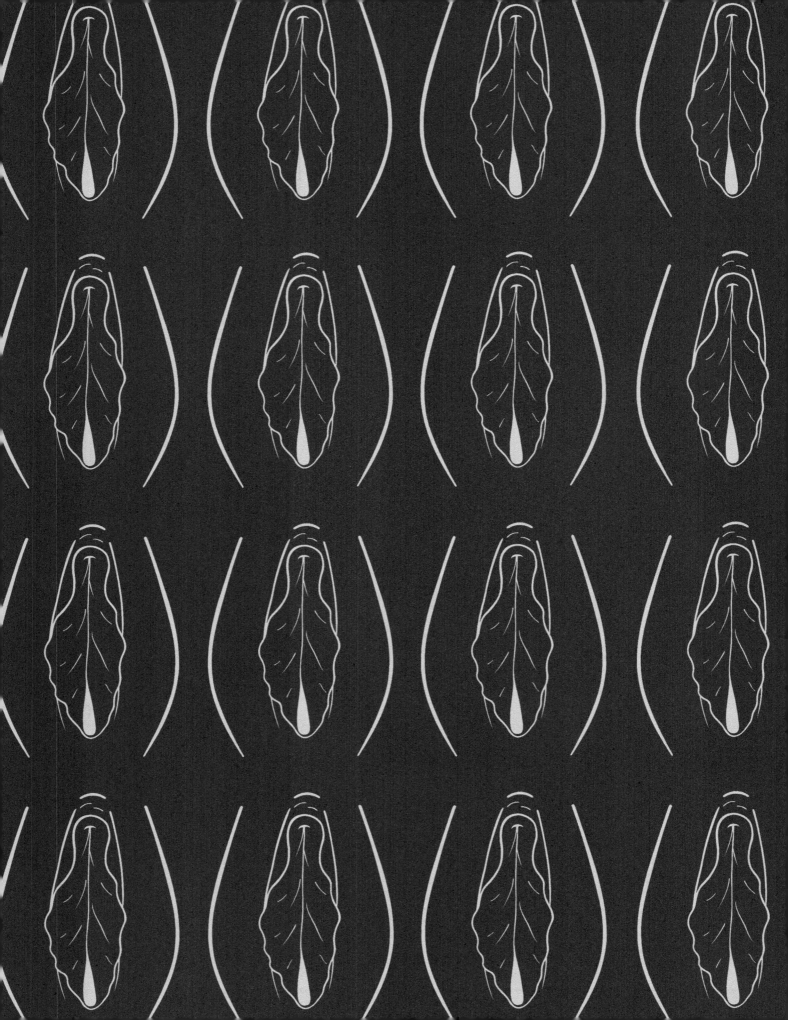

ZIPLINING

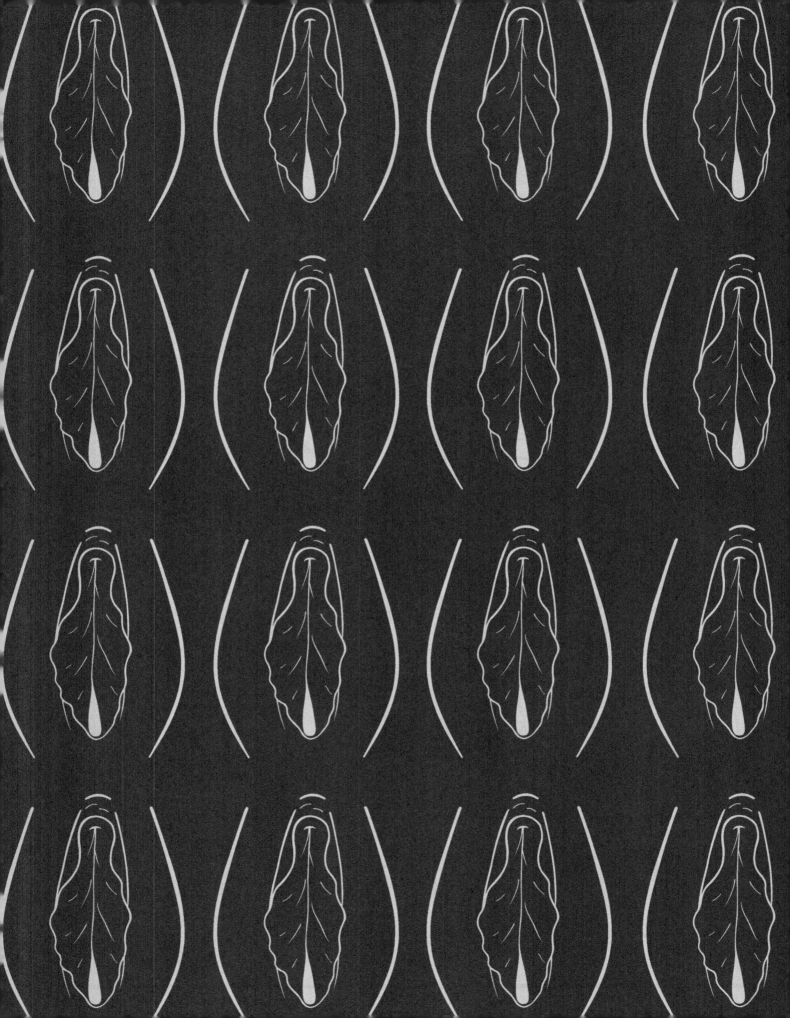

# COOKING COMPETITION

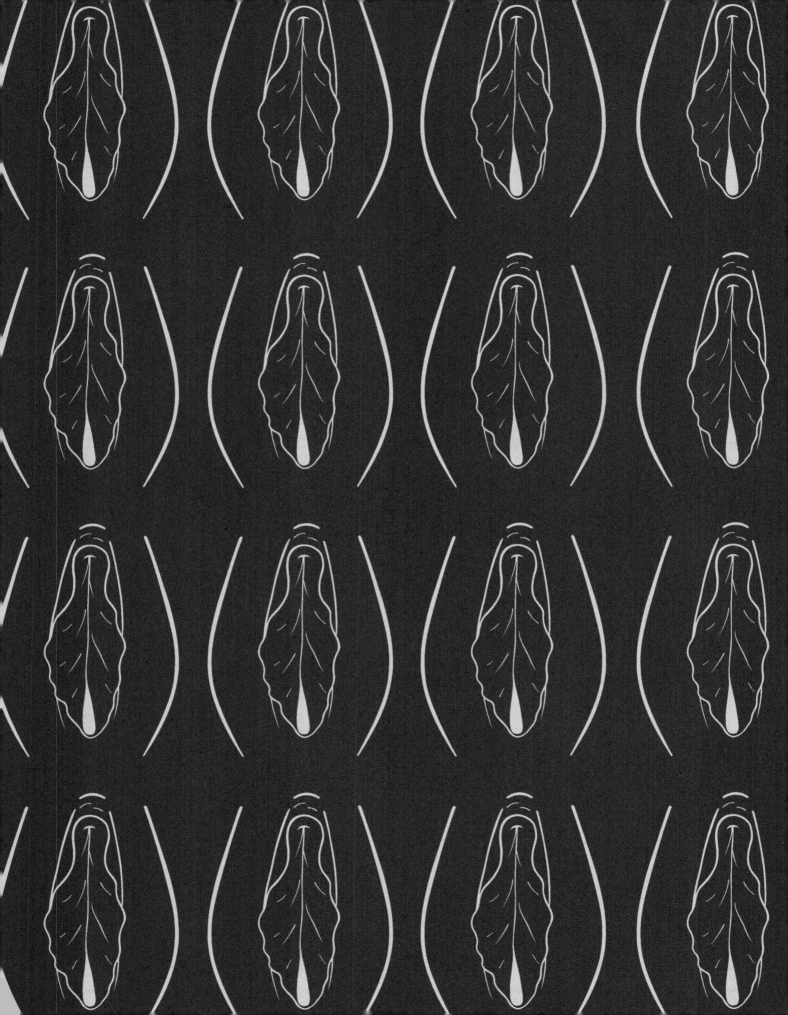

# ICE SKATING

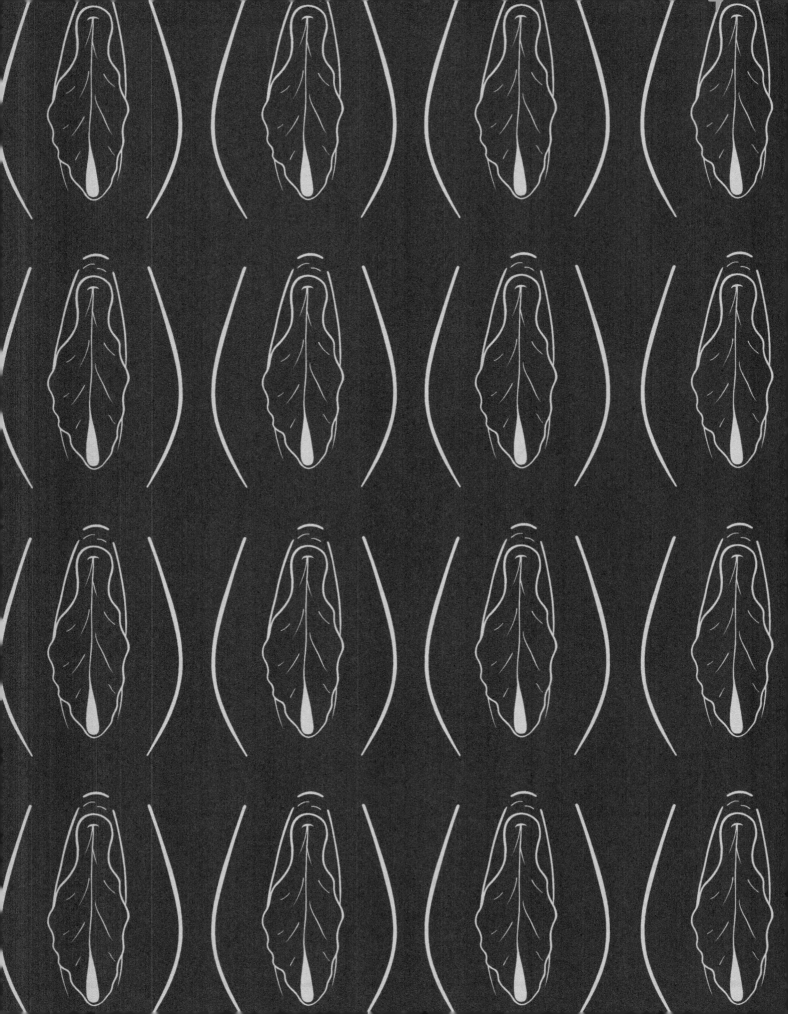

# SNOW
# SKIING

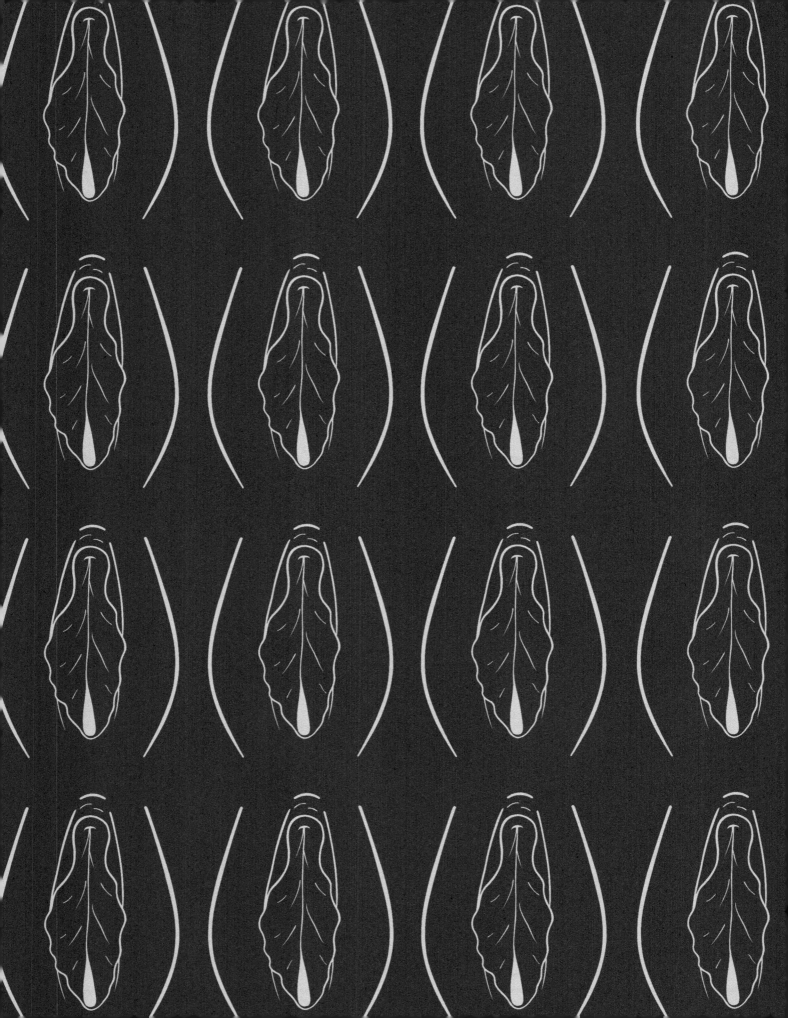

START
5
12

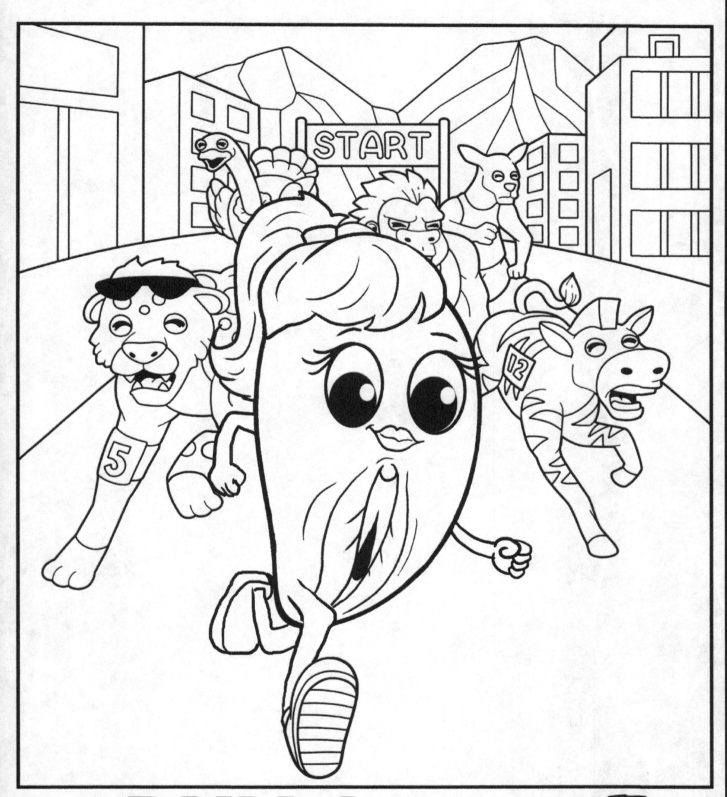

# RUN A MARATHON

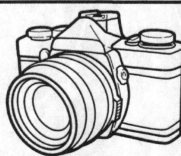

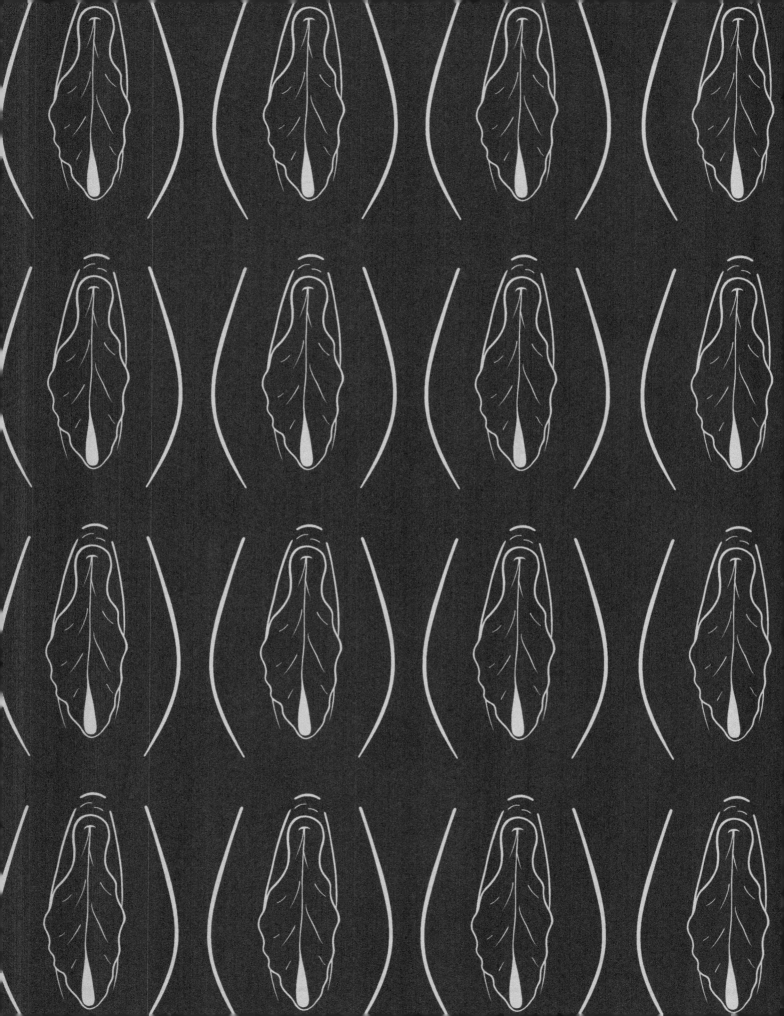

BOXING

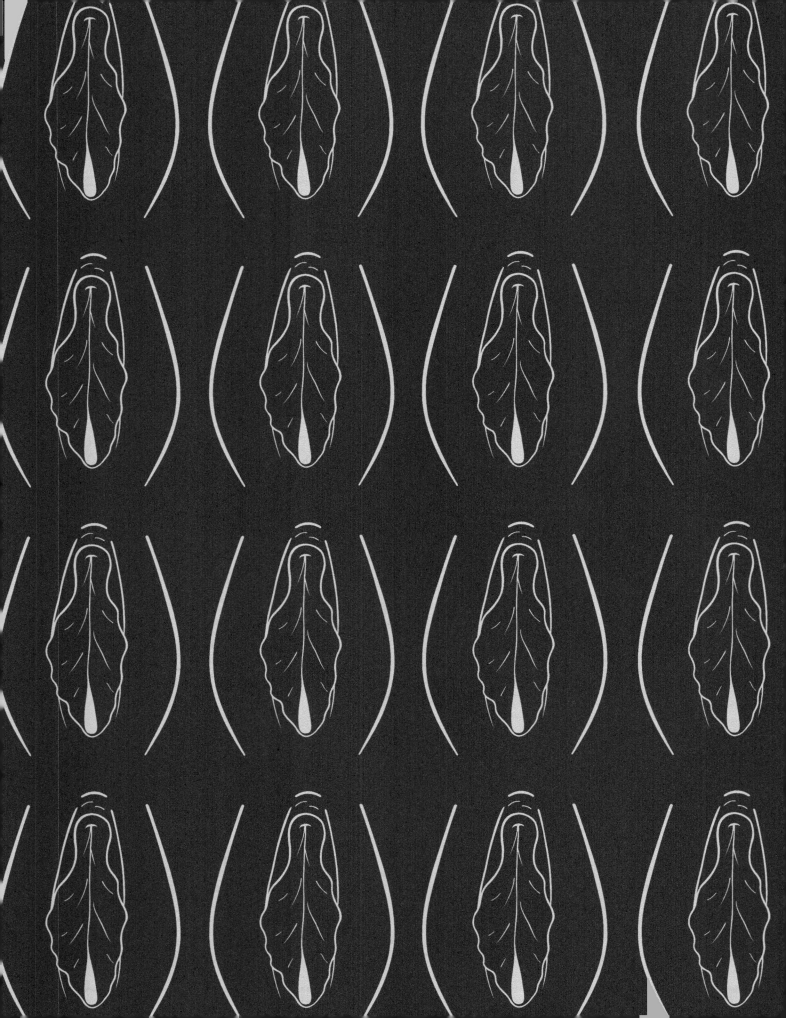

# FENCING

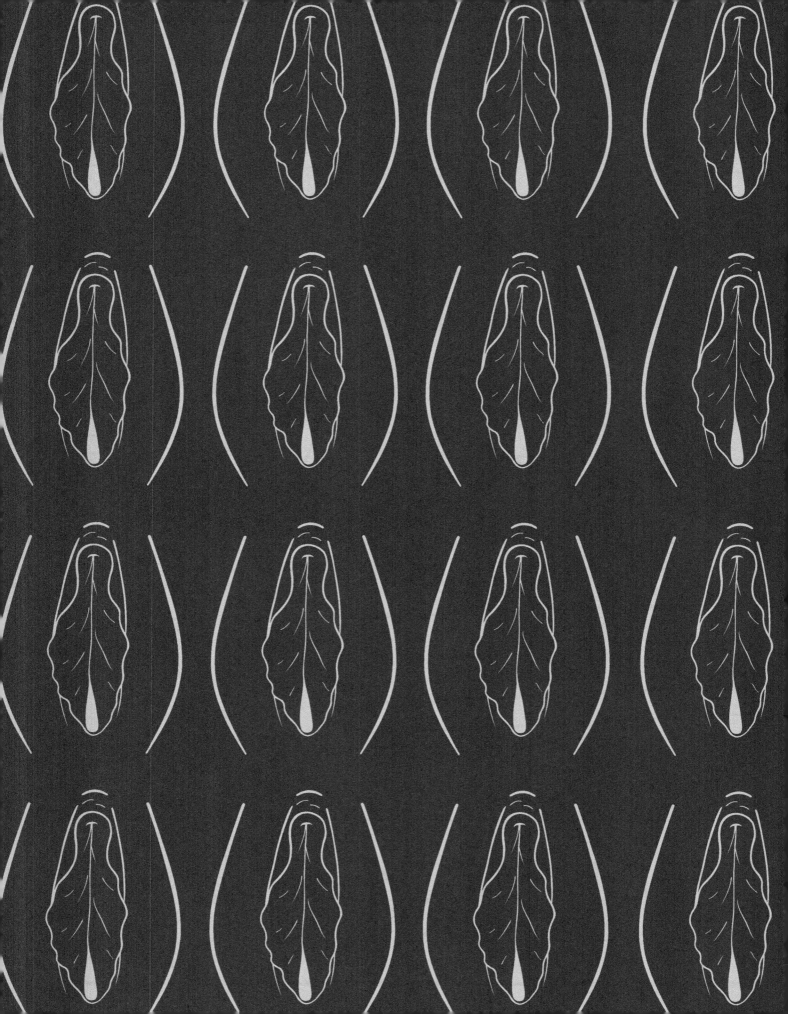

# JET SKIING

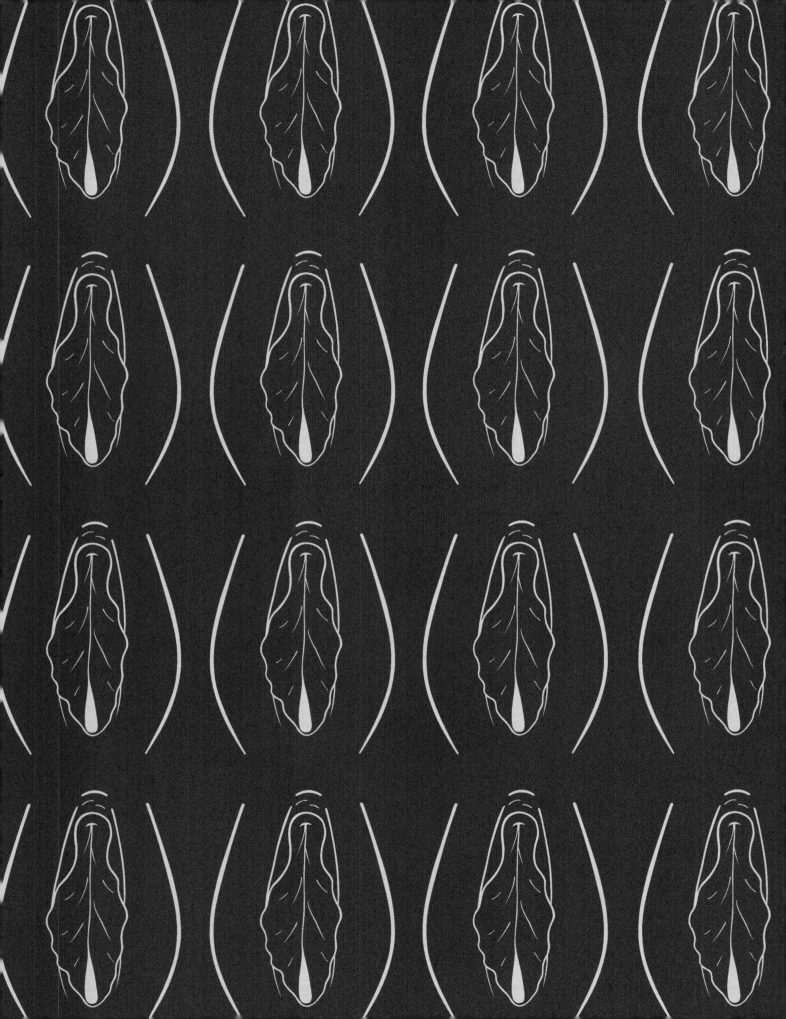

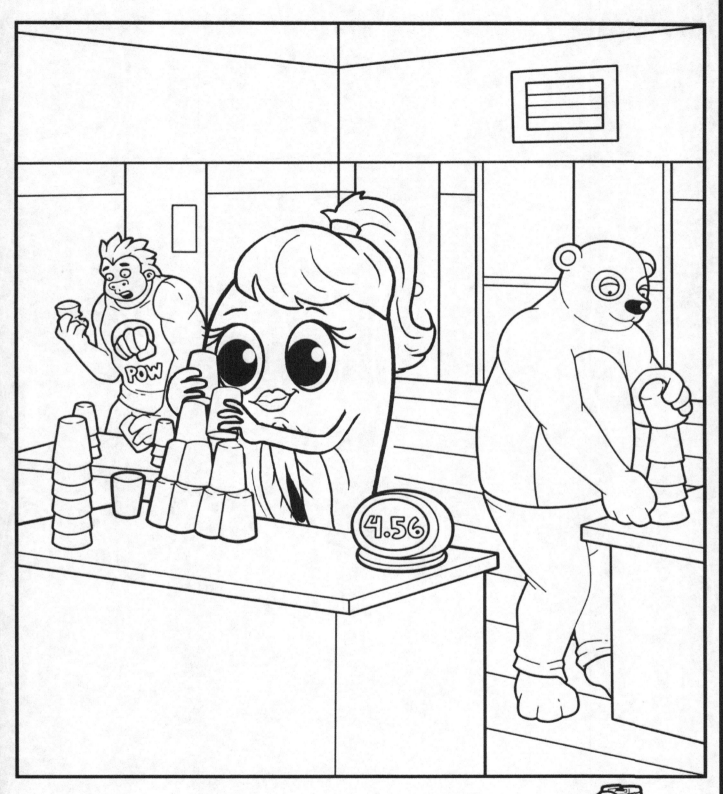

# CUP STACKING COMPETITION

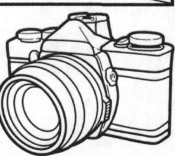

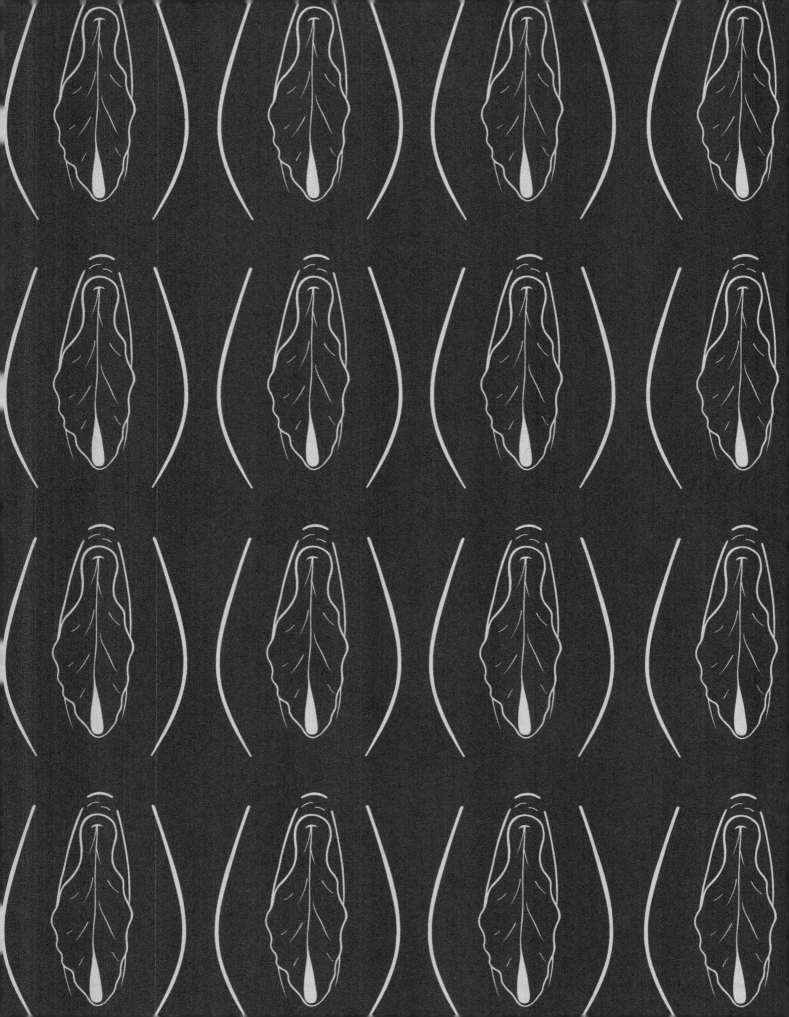

# POKER CHAMPION

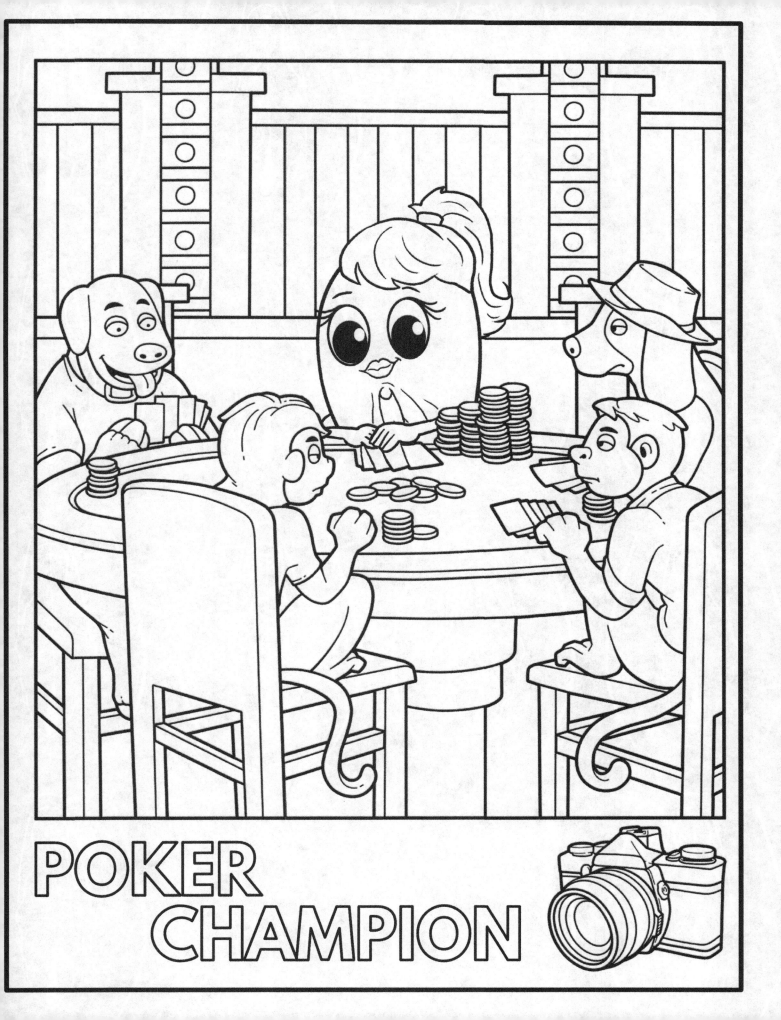

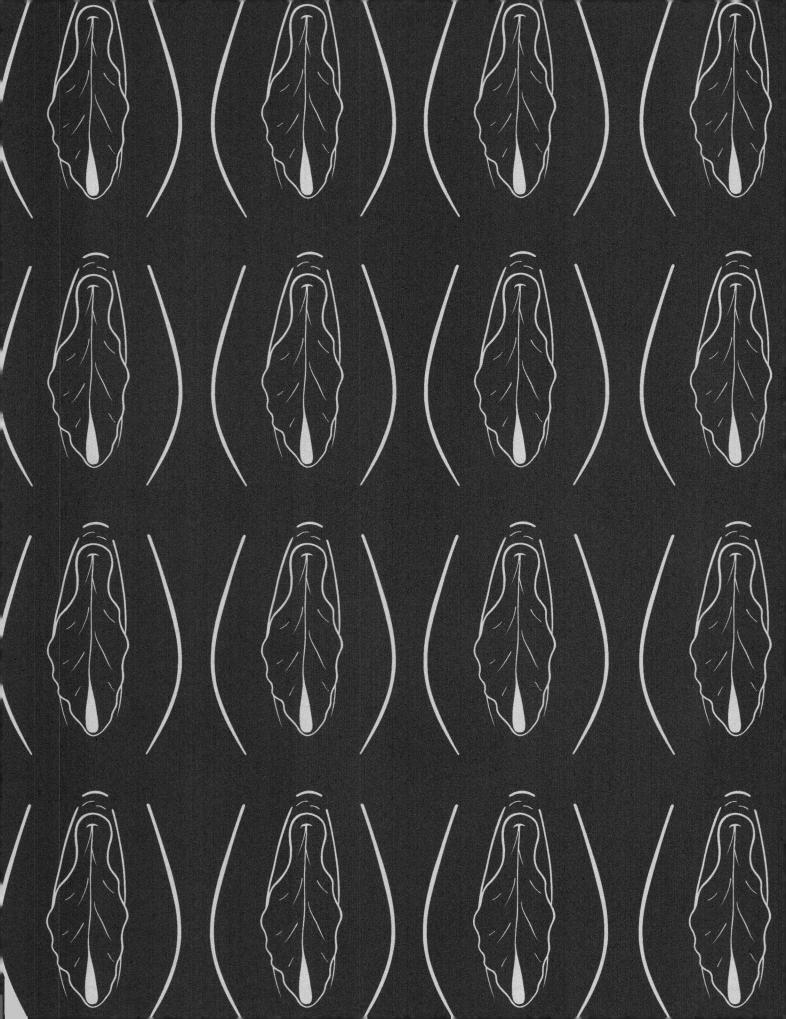

SINGING
KARAOKE

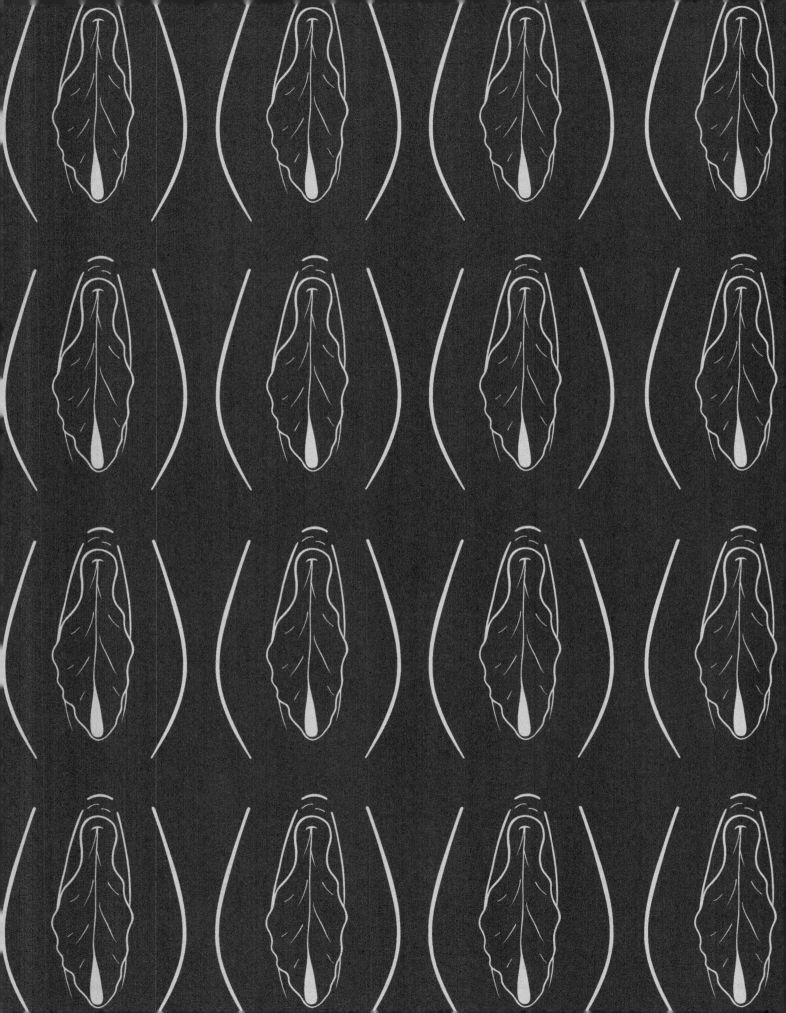

# PIRATING

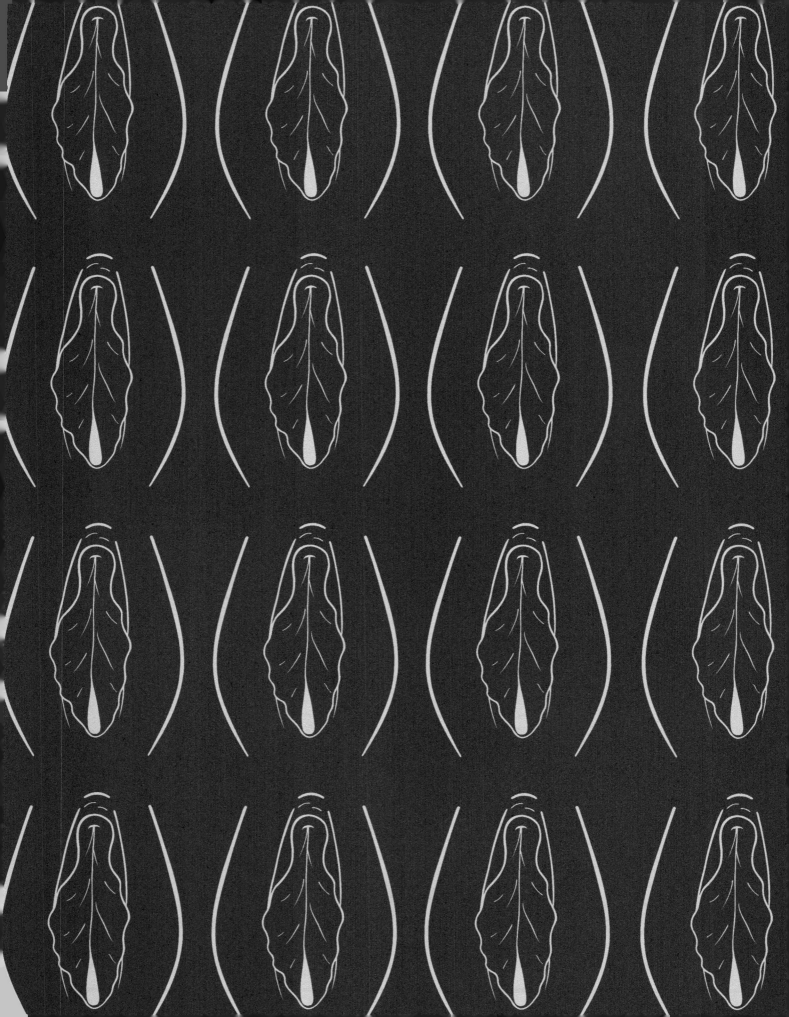

# BUNGEE
# JUMPING

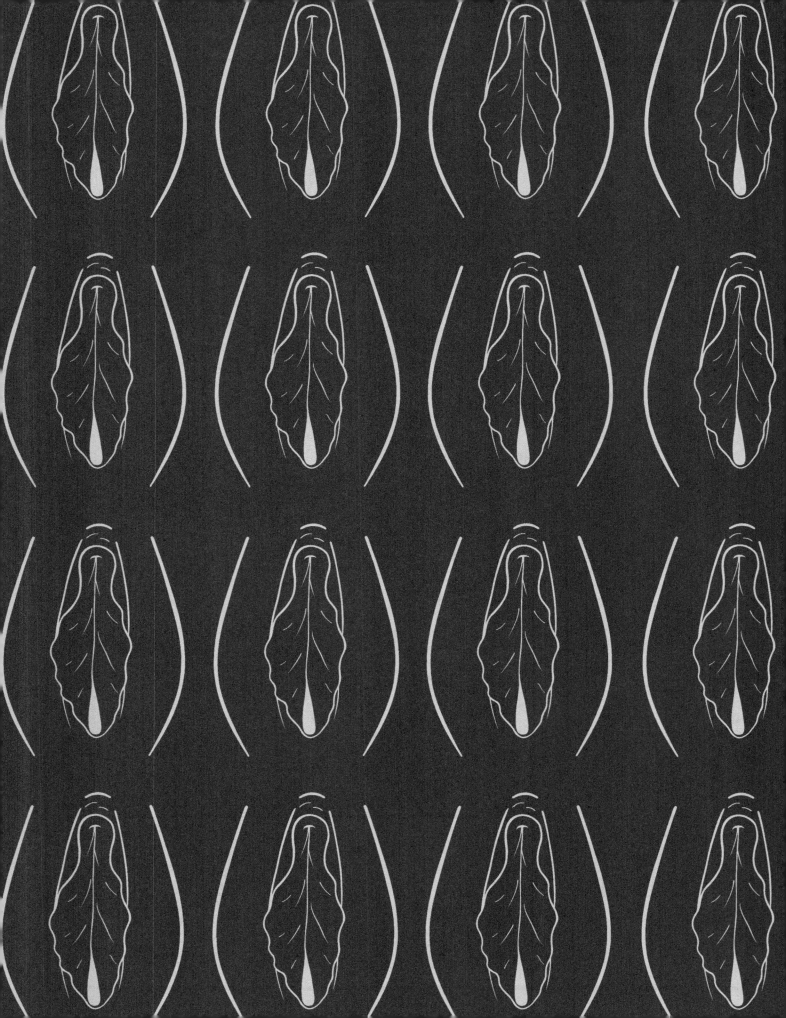

SCUBA
DIVING

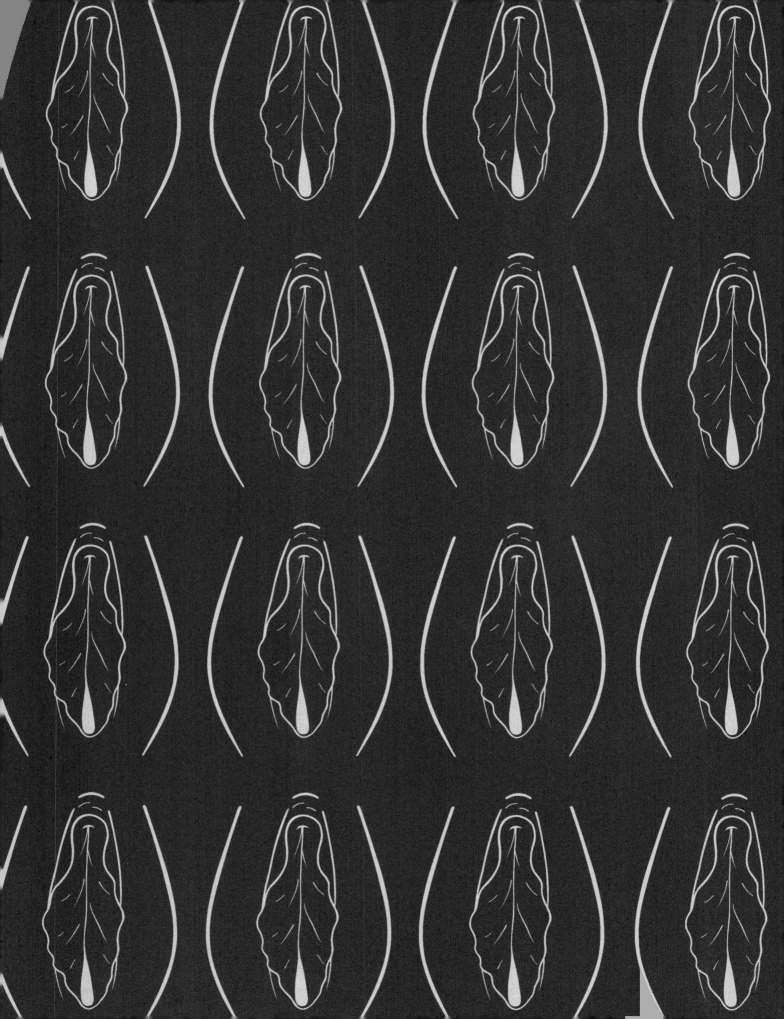

TRAPEZE
ARTIST

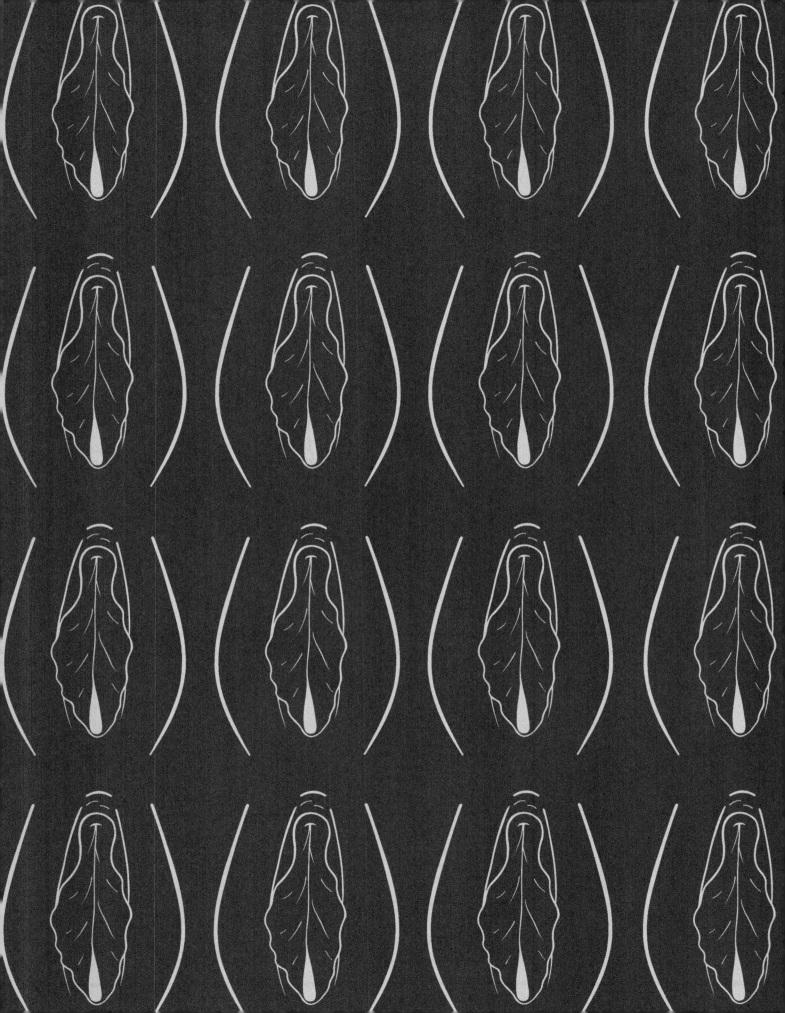

# BIKING ACROSS AMERICA

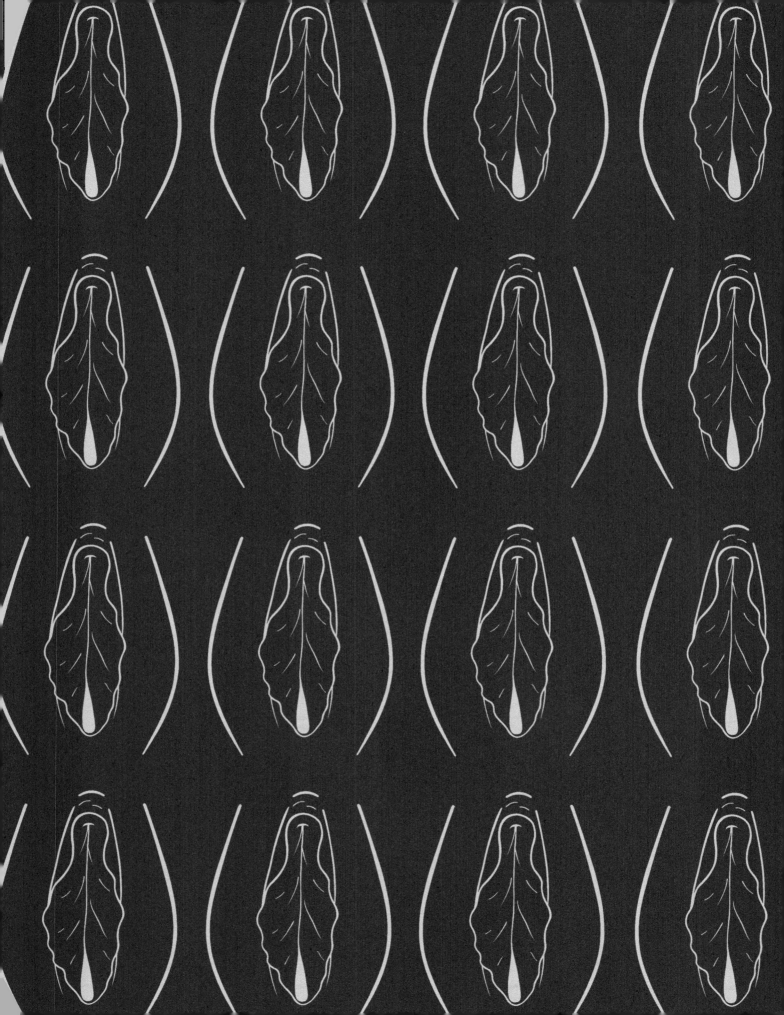

COW TIPPING

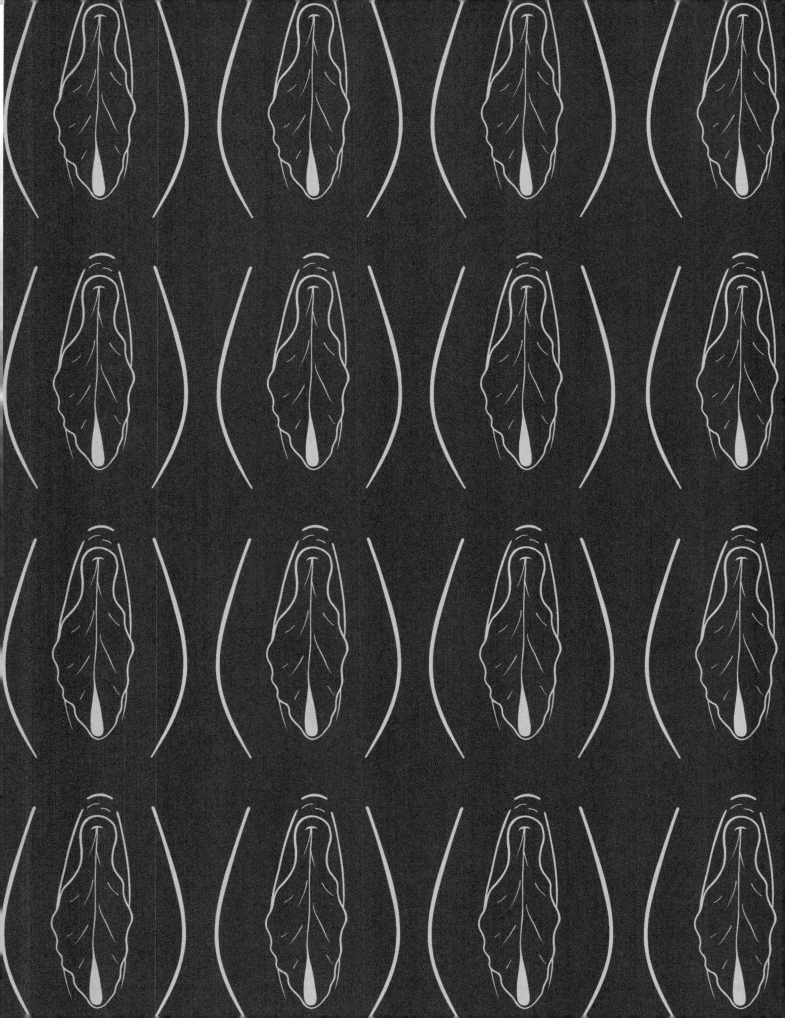

SKATEBOARDING

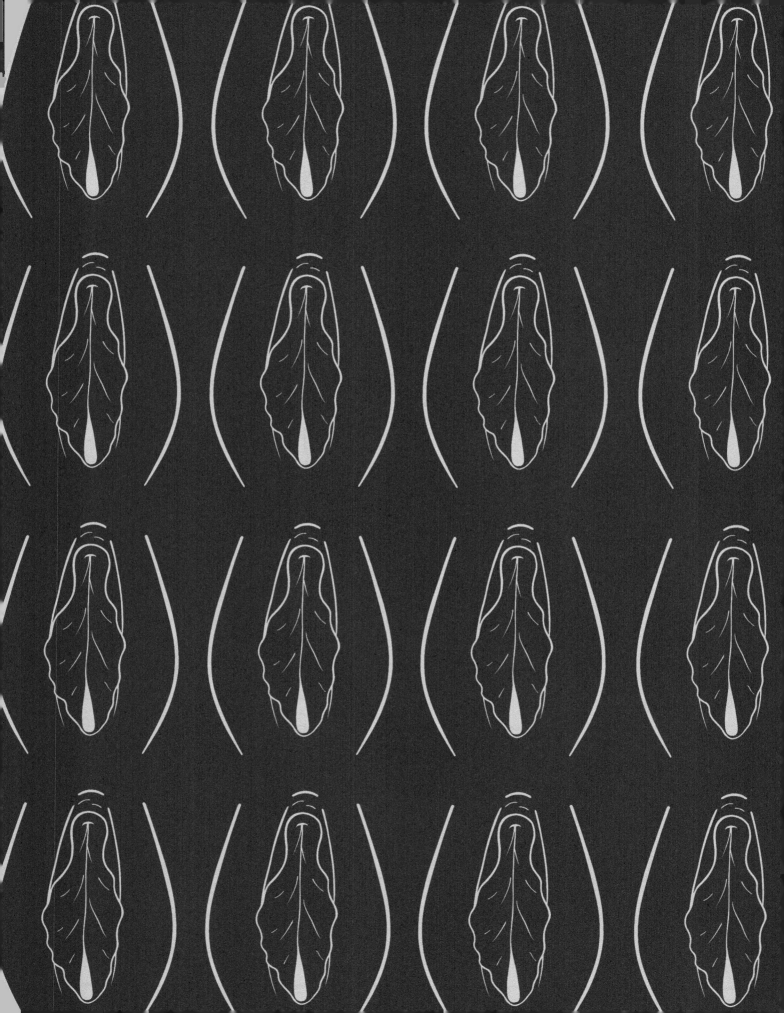

# MOVIE STAR

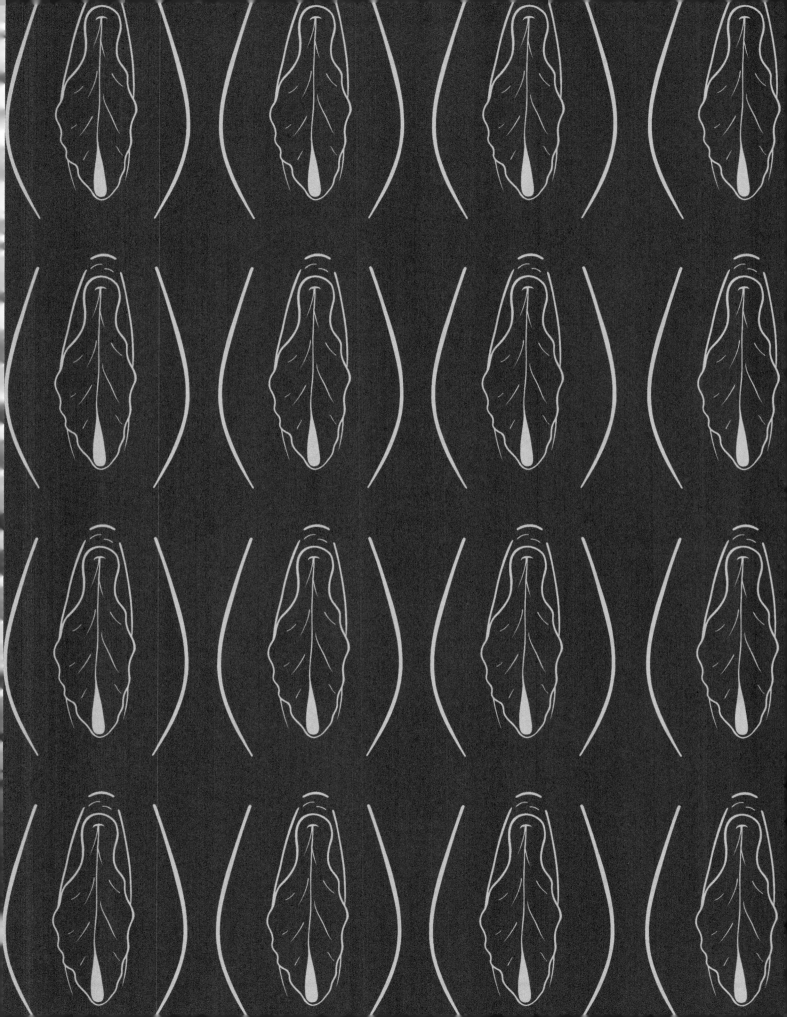

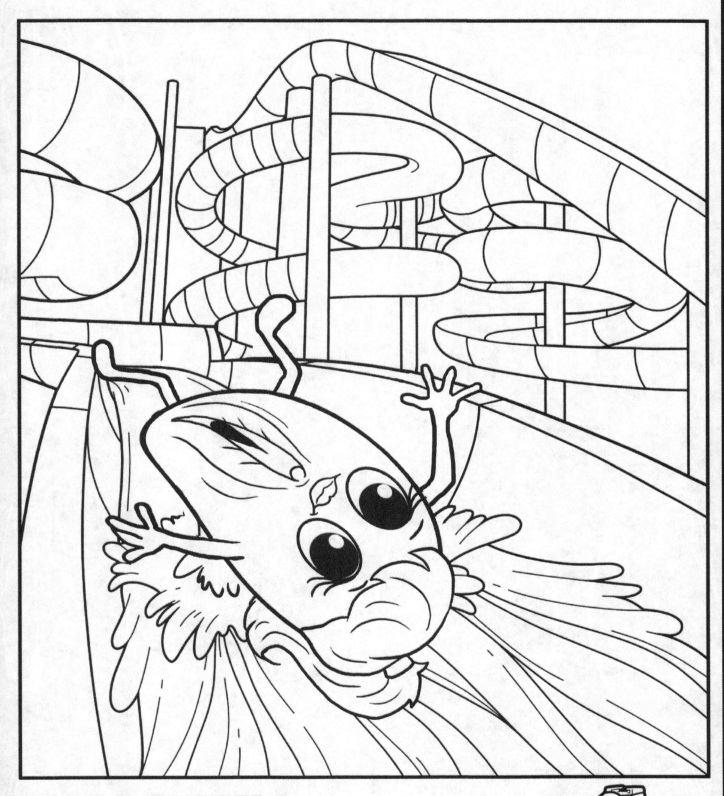

# WATER
# SLIDING

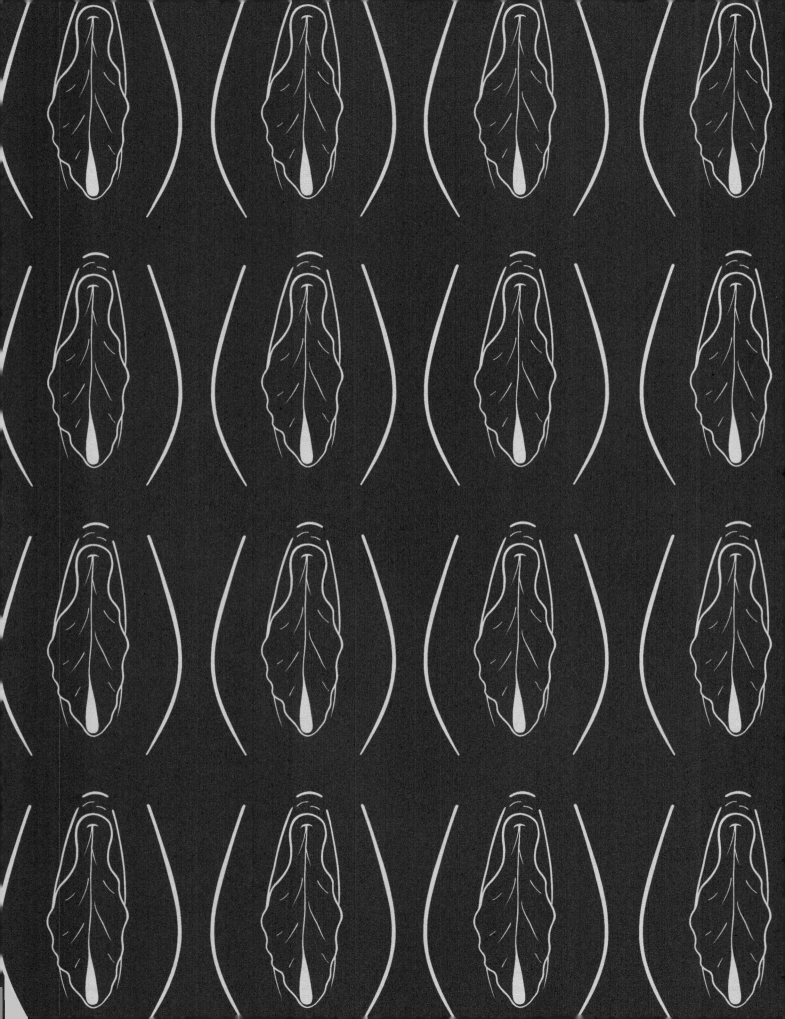

# ROLLER COASTER

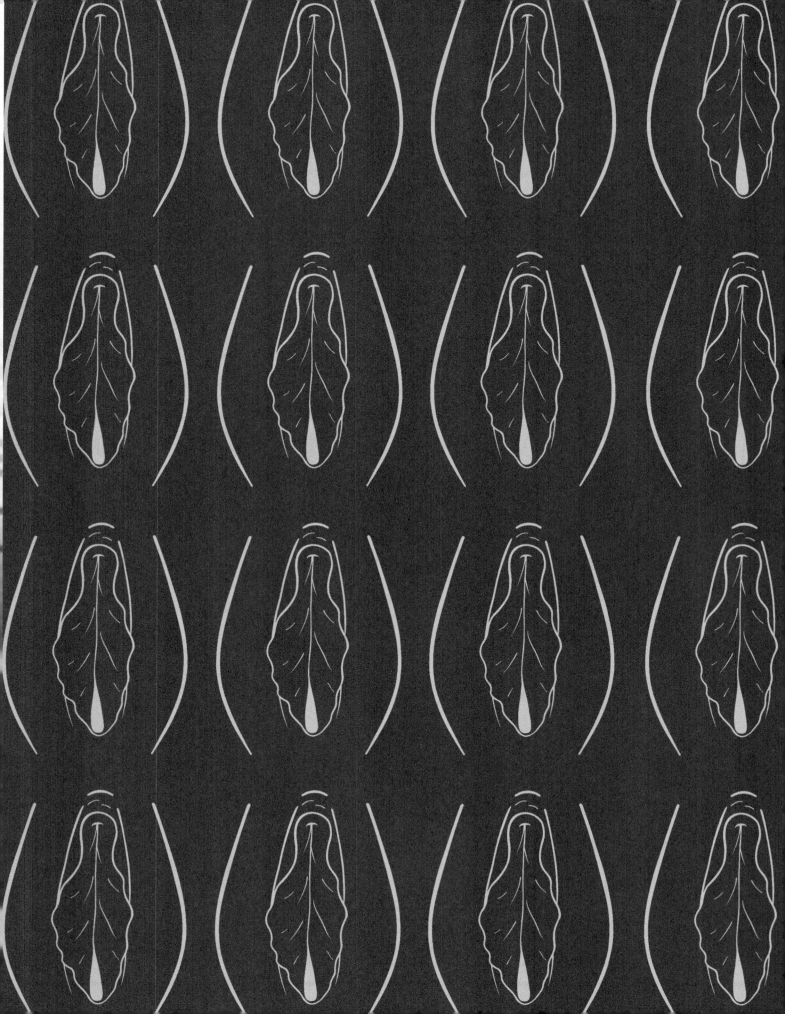

# TRY SOMETHING DIFFERENT!

**As a bonus, I offer you one page to color from each of the books:**


HALLOWEEN
STONER
COLORING BOOK


STONER
COLORING BOOK
FOR ADULTS

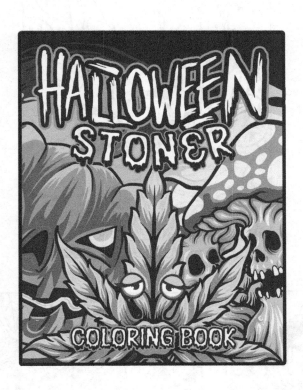

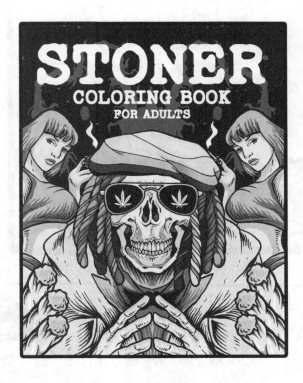

# Discover more:

Scan the QR CODE
or
type in your Amazon search bar:

ISBN: B09BZL94H5

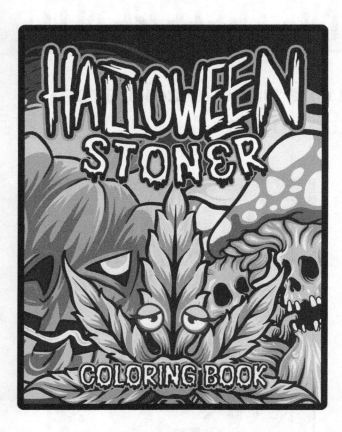

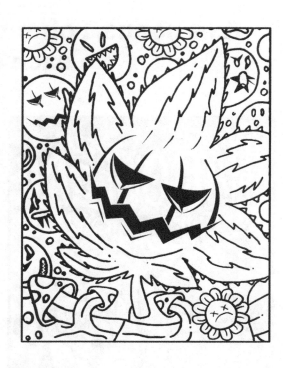

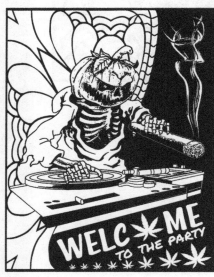

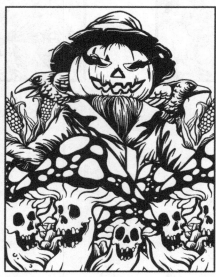

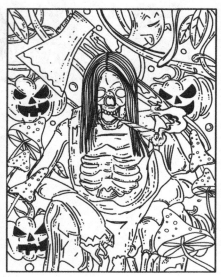

# Discover more:

Scan the QR CODE
or
type in your Amazon search bar:

ISBN: B09WYQ7R1S

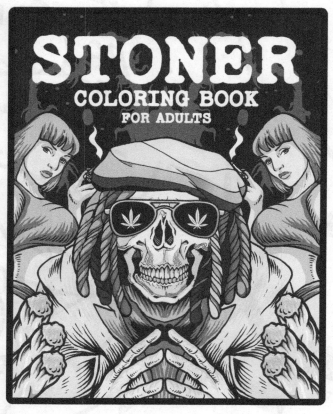

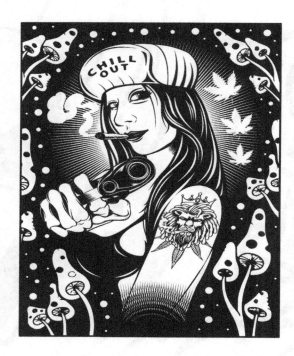

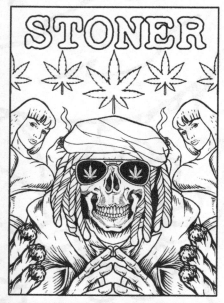

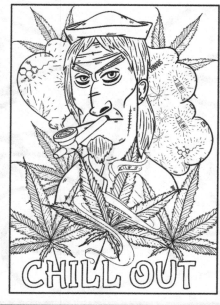

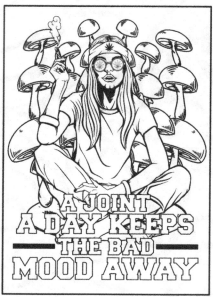

STONER

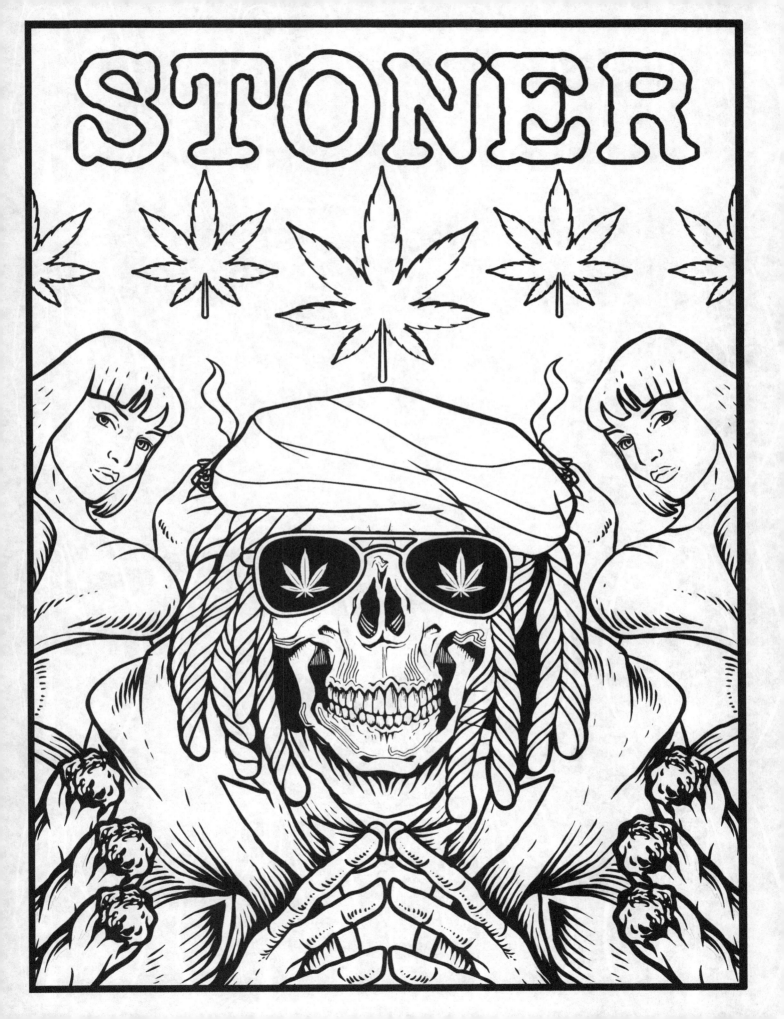

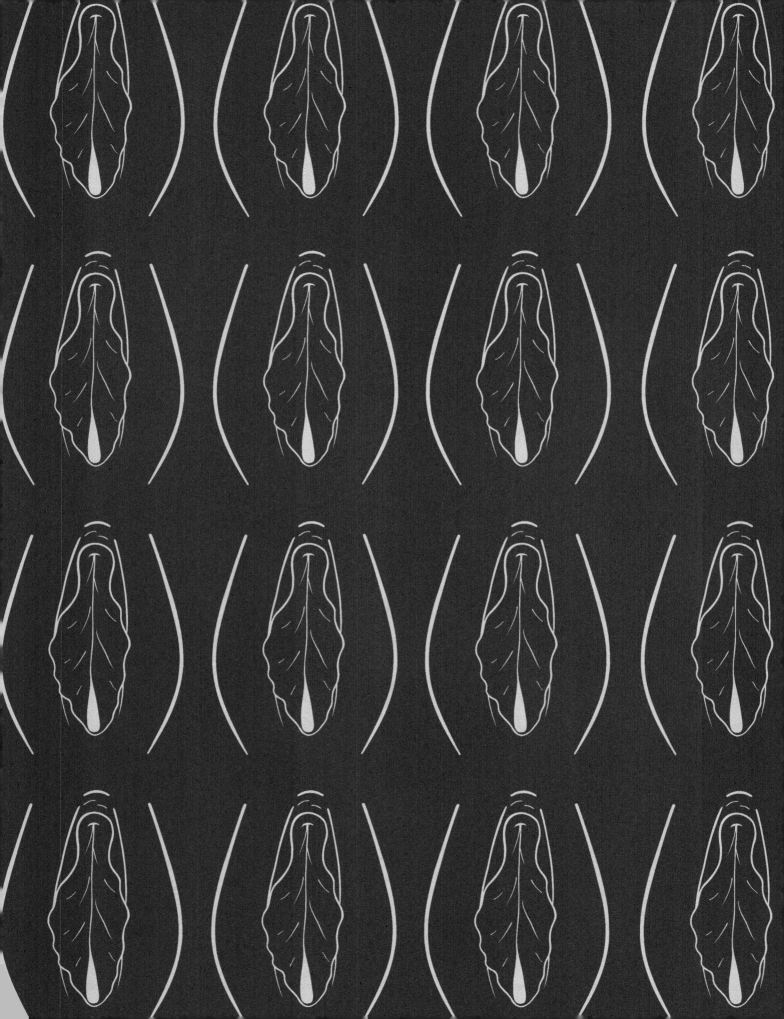

# THANK YOU

Just a note to say thank you your purchase from me.
I hope you enjoyed my product as much as I have
enjoyed creating it.

## If you want:

1. You can leave a review under this book on Amazon.

2. You can check out my other books by scan the QR
Code on the back cover.

3. You can follow my profile on Amazon and get New
Releases.

### Contact me:

books@relaxingcolorspress.com

### Website

www.relaxingcolorspress.com

Made in the USA
Las Vegas, NV
05 November 2023